1 Mary had a baby

F

spiritual
Carol gaily carol 21

Ma-ry had a ba-by, Yes Lord, Ma-ry had a ba-by, Yes my Lord.

tuned percussion (A, B♭, C′) plus **tambourine**

chime bar (F) plus **woodblock**

Ma-ry had a ba-by, Yes Lord, The peo-ple keep a-coming and the train done gone.

2 My ship sailed from China

traditional
Apusskidu 7

Indian bells (play at each ❋)

My ship sailed from Chi - na with a car - go of tea, All la - den with pre - sents for you and for me. They brought me a fan, just i - ma - gine my bliss when I fan my - self gai - ly like this, like this, like this, like this, like this.

cymbal
pp

The cymbal part can be a suspended cymbal with a wire brush, or a pair of cymbals clashed very softly. The Indian bells player should play as softly and delicately as possible.

This song includes F and F♯. F♯ is a semitone higher than F, halfway between F and G.

3 Heads, shoulders, knees and toes

traditional (There is a tavern in the town)
Okki-tokki-unga 1

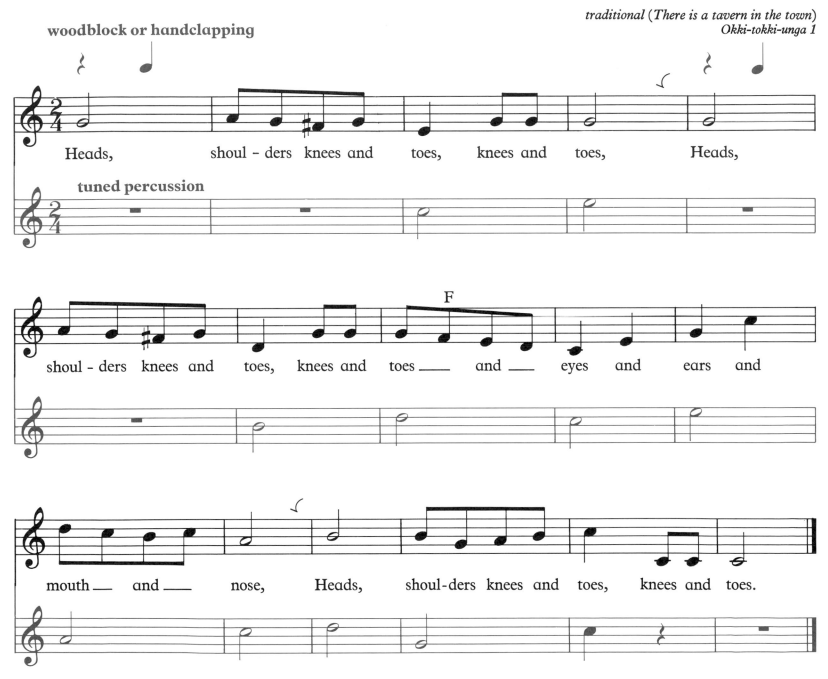

4 Morningtown ride

Malvina Reynolds
Apusskidu 25

smoothly, quietly

Train whis - tle blow - ing, makes a sleep - y noise.

tuned percussion or piano

guitar chords

C   F   C

Un – der – neath their blan - kets go all the girls and boys.

F   C   F   G

Rock - ing, rol - ling, ri - ding, out a - long the bay,

C   F   C

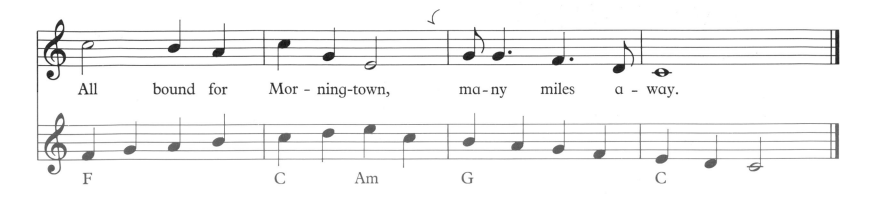

All　　bound for　Mor - ning-town,　　ma-ny　miles　a - way.

F　　　　　　　　C　　　　Am　　　G　　　　　　C

5 The drunken sailor

traditional shanty
The Jolly Herring 44

What shall we do with the drunk - en sai - lor,　What shall we do with the drunk - en sai - lor,

What shall we do with the drunk - en sai - lor,　ear - ly　in　the　morn - ing?

Hoo - ray　and　up　she　ri - ses,　Hoo - ray　and　up　she　ri - ses,

Hoo - ray　and　up　she　ri - ses,　ear - ly　in　the　morn - ing.

6 Where have all the flowers gone?

Pete Seeger
Alleluya 37

Where have all the flowers gone? Long time pas - sing.

tuned percussion (preferably doubled, e.g. soprano glockenspiel plus bass xylophone.)

guitar chords   C   Am   F   G

Where have all the flowers gone? Long time a - go.

C   Am   F   G

Where have all the flowers gone? Girls have picked them ev - 'ry one.

C   Am   F   G

When will they e-ver learn? When will they e-ver learn?

F   C   F   G   C

7 John Barleycorn

traditional
The Jolly Herring 34

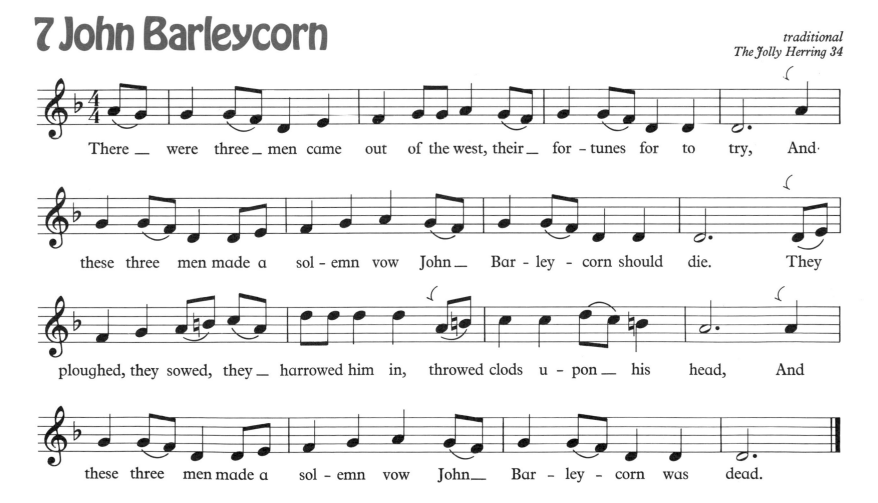

There _ were three _ men came out of the west, their _ for-tunes for to try, And these three men made a sol-emn vow John _ Bar-ley-corn should die. They ploughed, they sowed, they _ harrowed him in, throwed clods u-pon _ his head, And these three men made a sol-emn vow John _ Bar-ley-corn was dead.

8 Turn, turn, turn

words: *Ecclesiastes 3, vv 1-8, adapted by Pete Seeger*
music: *Pete Seeger*
Alleluya 32

9 Huron Indian carol

words: J. E. Middleton
music: traditional
Merrily to Bethlehem 5

Je - sus your king is born, Je - sus is born. In ex - cel - sis glo - ri - a!

10 The leaving of Liverpool

traditional
The Jolly Herring 48

guitar chords: C | F C | G

Fare thee well, the Prin - ce's — Land-ing Stage, Ri-ver Mer-sey, fare thee well, For I'm

C | F C | G C

bound for Ca - li - for - ni - ay, a place— that I know well. So —

G | F C | G

fare thee well, my own true love, When I re-turn u-ni-ted we will be. ——— It's not the

C | F C | G C

leav - ing of Li-ver-pool that grieves ——— me, but— darling when I think of thee.

11 Dance of the cuckoos

Marvin Hatley

staccato

Fine

D. C. al Fine

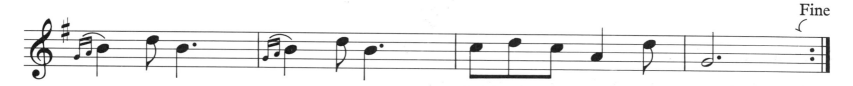

Percussion

Wooden sounds: xylophone, woodblock, claves etc.

And cuckoo sounds: instruments or voices or a mechanical cuckoo.

B♭

Sharps are higher, flats are lower.

C♯ is a semitone higher than C. B♭ is a semitone lower than B.
Play B, then B♭, and listen to the difference.

Play, very slowly:

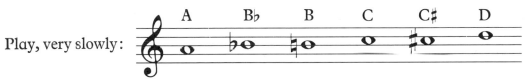

A B♭ B C C♯ D

12 The water is wide

traditional
The Jolly Herring 58

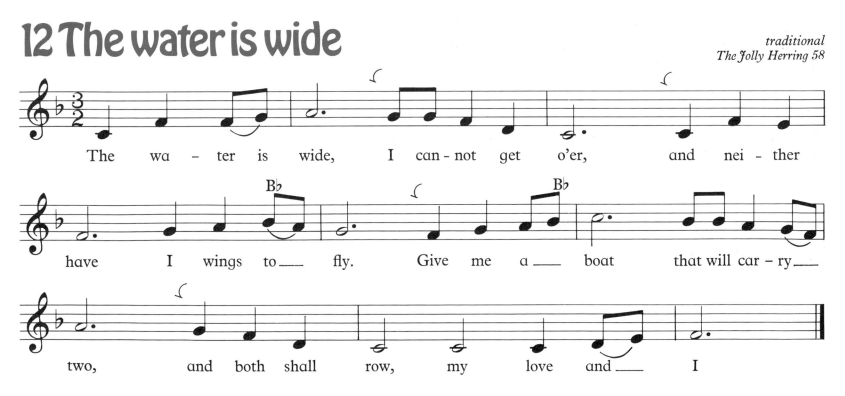

The wa – ter is wide, I can-not get o'er, and nei – ther

have I wings to ___ fly. Give me a ___ boat that will car – ry ___

two, and both shall row, my love and ___ I

13 It fell upon a summer day

words: Stopforde A. Brooke
music: H. Walford Davies
Someone's singing Lord 31

It ____ fell u - pon ____ a ____ sum - mer day, When

Je - sus walked in Ga - li - lee, The mo — thers from a

vil - lage ____ brought their chil - dren to his ____ knee.

2nd descant recorder

Bb

(↲) The breathing mark in brackets means: Breathe here if you have to, but carry on
without a breath if you can.

14 O Christmas tree

traditional German
Carol gaily carol 41

O Christmas tree, O Christmas tree, How love-ly are your branches. O

percussion

(Christmas tree,)

Choose a jingly, Christmasy instrument

Christmas tree, O Christmas tree, How love-ly are your bran - ches. In

beauty green they'll always grow through summer sun and win - ter snow. O

tuned percussion (F, G, A)

15 Patapan

words: Percy Dearmer
music: traditional French
Merrily to Bethlehem 42

2nd
descant recorder
or
tuned percussion

low - register
tuned percussion

or **piano**

drum or **tambourine** — etc

Wil – lie   take   your   lit – tle   drum. With your whist – le,

Ro – bin,   come. When   we   hear   the   fife   and   drum,   tu – re – lu – re –

lu,   pa - ta - pa - ta - pan,   When   we   hear   the   fife   and

drum,   Christ - mas   should   be ___   fro - lic - some.

16 Standing in the rain

Sydney Carter
Carol gaily carol 7

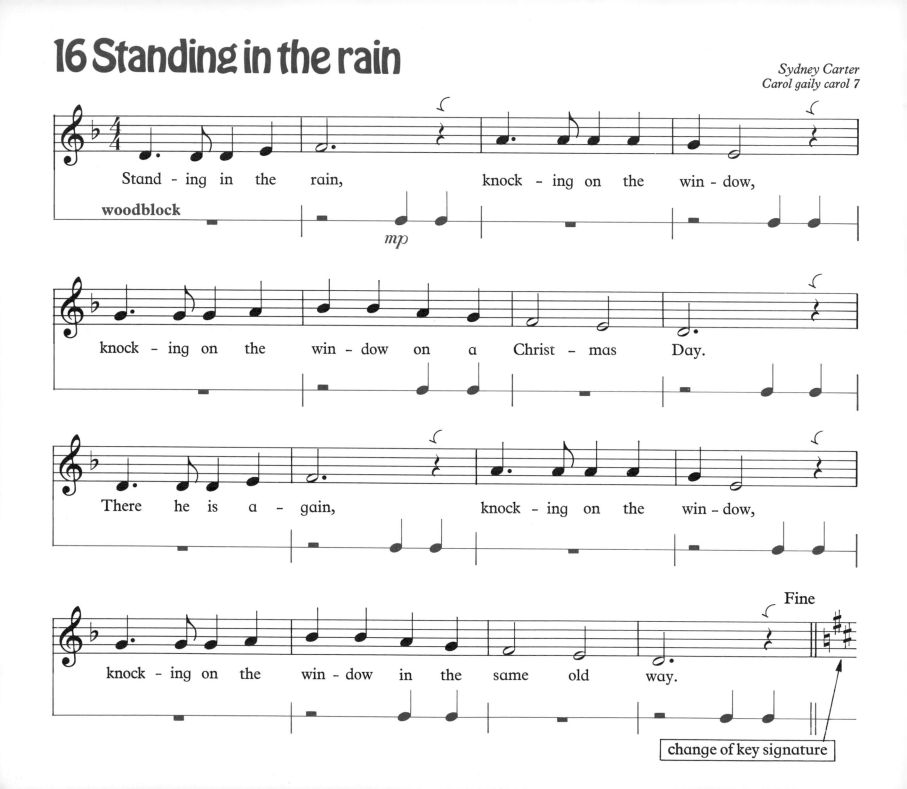

No use knock - ing on the win – dow.   There is

suspended cymbal (with hard beater)

damp with hand—make the sound as short as possible   *f*

no - thing we can do sir.   All the beds are booked al -

D. C. al Fine

rea - dy,   there is no - thing left for you sir.

17 Choucoune (2nd recorder part)

Haitian
Ta-ra-ra boom-de-ay 21 (in F)

descant recorder 1 (tune)

Have you heard the song of the mock - ing bird?

descant recorder 2 (harmony)

A♯
(same as B♭)

A

Have you heard the song of the mock - ing bird?

When you sad and blue, then he mock at you, He sing high a-bove, and he laugh at love.

Oh I heard his tune by the Hai-tian moon, when I lost my Choucoune.

18 This old man

traditional
Okki-tokki-unga 39

This old man, he played one, he played nick nack on my thumb, With a

tuned percussion

nick nack paddy whack, give a dog a bone, this old man came rol – ling home.

19 Down in Demerara

traditional (student song)
Apusskidu 46

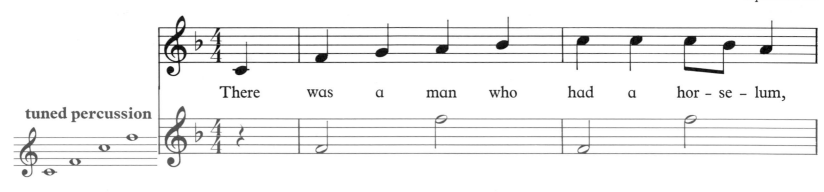

There was a man who had a hor - se - lum,

tuned percussion

had a hor - se - lum, had a hor - se - lum, Was a man who

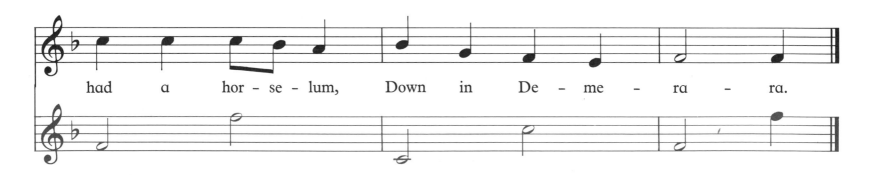

had a hor - se - lum, Down in De - me - ra - ra.

20 Gobbolino the witch's cat

Graham Westcott
Apusskidu 53

One fine night in a witch-'s cavern two lit-tle kit-tens rolled

on - to the floor. One, called Soo-ti-ca, was black all o-ver, the

change of key signature

o-ther, Gob-bo-li-no, had one white paw.

Who'll give a home to a kit-ten? _____

Who'll give a home to a cat? Gob-bo-li-no you may

call me, _____ I want just a fire and a mat.

21 Mango walk

traditional
Ta-ra-ra boom-de-ay 20

My bro-ther did-a tell me that you go man-go walk, you

2nd descant recorder

go man-go walk, you go man-go walk, My bro-ther did-a tell me that you

go man-go walk and steal all the num-ber 'le-ven.

Fine

low C♯

The bottom hole must be only half covered.

Most recorders divide this hole into two small holes:

To play low C♯ cover just one of the small holes, the one nearest the little finger:

22 Linstead Market

traditional Jamaican
Ta-ra-ra boom-de-ay 19

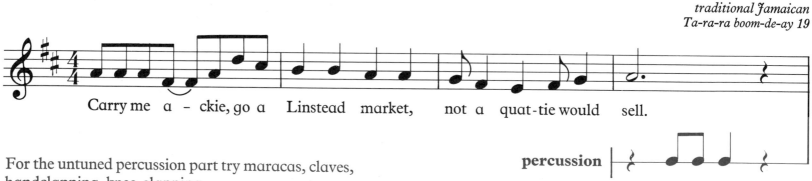

Carry me a – ckie, go a Linstead market, not a quat-tie would sell.

percussion

For the untuned percussion part try maracas, claves, handclapping, knee-slapping. . .
Which sounds best ?

Car - ry me a - ckie, go a Linstead mar - ket, not a quat - tie would sell.

Lord, not a mite, not a bite, what a Sa - tur - day night!

tuned percussion

Lord, not a mite, not a bite, What a Sa - tur - day night!

Where to breathe: at the rests. Rests nearly always make good breathing places, so it isn't really necessary to put a breathing mark over a rest.

23 Sans Day carol

words: collated by Percy Dearmer
music: traditional Cornish
Merrily to Bethlehem 32

Now the hol-ly bears a ber-ry as white as the milk, and ___

tuned percussion (D, E, F♯, A, B)

Ma - ry bore ___ Je - sus who was wrapped up in silk. And ___

Ma - ry bore ___ Je - sus Christ our Sa - viour for to be, and the

first tree in the green-wood it was the hol - ly, hol - ly, hol -

- ly, and the first tree in the green-wood it was the hol - ly.

24 Merrily to Bethlehem

words: Polish, tr. Jan Sliwinski
music: adapted by Arnold Bax
Merrily to Bethlehem 17

Mer - ri - ly to Bethlehem, ter - li, ter - low, come the shepherds singing and their pipes they blow.

Glo - ry to God in heaven, Glo - ry to God in heaven, and on earth, peace to men.

25 Kum ba yah (2nd recorder part)

traditional
Someone's singing Lord 23

recorder 1

Kum ba yah, my Lord, kum ba yah, Kum ba yah, my Lord, kum ba

recorder 2

guitar chords: D   G   D   D   G
                                            (or F#m) (or Em)

yah, Kum ba yah, my Lord, kum ba yah, O Lord __ kum ba yah

A   D   G   D   A   D   A   D
                                          (or G)

Always adapt and arrange to fit your resources. For instance, the 2nd recorder
part might be hummed softly, with just one or two recorders playing the tune. . .
There's a percussion accompaniment in book 1 of *Abracadabra Recorder*, and a
piano accompaniment in *Someone's singing, Lord*, and more ideas and arrangements
in other books.

26 Brown girl in the ring

traditional Caribbean
Mango Spice 38

descant recorder 1 (harmony)

descant recorder 2 (tune)

There's a brown girl in the ring, tra la la la la, there's a

brown girl in the ring, tra la la la la, There's a brown girl in the ring,

tra la la la la, For she like su - gar and I like plum.

Acknowledgements

We are most grateful to all the teachers and advisers who have helped us to prepare this book. Our particular thanks to Leonora Davies, Catherine Johnson, Martin Sheldon and Cynthia Watson.

The following copyright owners have kindly granted their permission for the reprinting of words and music:

Chappell Music Ltd and International Music Publications for 24 'Merrily to Bethlehem', © 1944 Chappell & Co Ltd.

Westminster Music Ltd for 16 'Standing in the rain'.

Essex Music and Fall River Music Inc for 6 'Where have all the flowers gone', ©Harmony Music Ltd, ©1961 Fall River Music Inc.

TRO Essex Music Ltd, Essex Music of Australia Pty Ltd and The Richmond Organization for 8 'Turn turn turn', ©1962 Melody Trails Inc, New York. Reproduced by permission of TRO Essex Music Ltd.

Alfred Lengnick & Co Ltd for the words of 9 'Huron Indian carol'.

Leosong Copyright Service Ltd for 4 'Morningtown ride', ©Amadeo Brio Music Inc.

Lewis Music Publishing Co Inc for 17 'Choucoune'.

Oxford University Press for 22 'Linstead Market', the words of 15 'Patapan' and 23 'Sans Day carol' and the music of 13 'It fell upon a summer day'.

H. & R. Shekerjian for the words of 14 'O Christmas tree'.

Southern Music Publishing Co Ltd, Southern Music Publishing Co (Australasia) Pty Ltd and Southern Music Publishing Co (S.A.) Pty Ltd for 11 'Dance of the cuckoos', ©1932 Southern Music Publishing Co Inc. Liber-Southern Ltd, 8 Denmark St, London WC2.

Graham Westcott for 20 'Gobbolino, the witch's cat'.

Every effort has been made to trace and acknowledge copyright owners. If any right has been omitted, the publishers offer their apologies and will rectify this in subsequent editions following notification.